CROWD

HOIST

SWING

To download your free audiobook, visit

www.hmhbooks.com/freedownloads

Access code: maryanne

MIKE MULLIGAN
AND HIS
STEAM SHOVEL

STORY AND PICTURES BY VIRGINIA LEE BURTON

HOUGHTON MIFFLIN HARCOURT

BOSTON   NEW YORK

The Library of Congress Catalog Card Number 39-30335

ISBN: 978-395-16961-5 hardcover
ISBN: 978-0-395-25939-8 paperback
ISBN: 978-0-544-27992-6 hardcover reissue

Manufactured in China
SCP 10 9 8 7 6 5 4 3 2 1

4500481665

TO

MIKE

Mike Mulligan had a steam shovel,
a beautiful red steam shovel.
Her name was Mary Anne.
Mike Mulligan was very proud of Mary Anne.
He always said that she could dig as much in a day
as a hundred men could dig in a week,
but he had never been quite sure
that this was true.

3

Mike Mulligan and Mary Anne
	had been digging together
		for years and years.
Mike Mulligan took such good care
	of Mary Anne
		she never grew old.

It was Mike Mulligan and Mary Anne
and some others
who dug the great canals
for the big boats
to sail through.

It was Mike Mulligan and
Mary Anne
and some others
who cut through
the high mountains
so that the trains
could go through.

It was Mike Mulligan and Mary Anne
and some others
who lowered the hills
and straightened the curves

to make the long highways
for the automobiles.

It was Mike Mulligan
and Mary Anne
and some others
who smoothed out the ground
and filled in the holes

to make the landing fields
for the airplanes.

And it was Mike Mulligan
and Mary Anne
and some others
who dug the deep holes
for the cellars
of the tall skyscrapers
in the big cities.
When people used to stop
and watch them,
Mike Mulligan and Mary Anne
used to dig a little faster
and a little better.
The more people stopped,
the faster and better they dug.
Some days they would keep
as many as thirty-seven trucks
busy taking away the dirt they had dug.

Then along came
  the new gasoline shovels
    and the new electric shovels
      and the new Diesel motor shovels
        and took all the jobs away from the steam shovels.

Mike Mulligan
and Mary Anne
were

VERY

SAD.

All the other steam shovels
were being sold for junk,
or left out in old gravel pits
to rust and fall apart.
Mike loved Mary Anne.
He couldn't do that to her.

He had taken
such good care of her
that she could still dig
as much in a day
as a hundred men
could dig in a week;
at least he thought she could
but he wasn't quite sure.
Everywhere they went
the new gas shovels
and the new electric shovels
and the new Diesel motor shovels
had all the jobs. No one wanted
Mike Mulligan and Mary Anne any more.
Then one day Mike read in a newspaper that the town
of Popperville was going to build a new town hall.
'We are going to dig the cellar of that town hall,'
said Mike to Mary Anne, and off they started.

They left the canals
    and the railroads
      and the highways
        and the airports
          and the big cities
            where no one wanted them any more
              and went away out in the country.

They crawled along slowly
   up the hills and down the hills
      till they came to the little town
         of Popperville.

When they got there they found that the selectmen
were just deciding who should dig the cellar for the new town hall.
Mike Mulligan spoke to Henry B. Swap, one of the selectmen.
'I heard,' he said, 'that you are going
to build a new town hall. Mary Anne and I
will dig the cellar for you in just one day.'
'What!' said Henry B. Swap. 'Dig a cellar in a day!
It would take a hundred men at least a week
to dig the cellar for our new town hall.'
'Sure,' said Mike, 'but Mary Anne can dig as much in a day
as a hundred men can dig in a week.'
Though he had never been quite sure that this was true.
Then he added,
'If we can't do it, you won't have to pay.'
Henry B. Swap thought that this would be
an easy way to get part of the cellar dug for nothing,
so he smiled in rather a mean way
and gave the job of digging the cellar of the new town hall
to Mike Mulligan and Mary Anne.

They started in
 early the next morning
  just as the sun was coming up.
   Soon a little boy came along.
    'Do you think you will finish by sundown?'
     he said to Mike Mulligan.
      'Sure,' said Mike, 'if you stay and watch us.
       We always work faster and better
        when someone is watching us.'
         So the little boy stayed to watch.

Then Mrs. McGillicuddy,
Henry B. Swap,
and the Town Constable
came over to see
what was happening,
and they stayed to watch.

Mike Mulligan
and Mary Anne
dug a little faster
and a little better.

This gave the little boy a good idea.

He ran off and told the postman with the morning mail,

the telegraph boy on his bicycle,

the milkman with his cart and horse,

the doctor on his way home,

and the farmer and his family

coming into town for the day,

and they all stopped and stayed to watch.

That made Mike Mulligan and Mary Anne

dig a little faster and a little better.

They finished the first corner

neat and square . . .

but the sun was getting higher.

Clang! Clang! Clang!
 The Fire Department arrived.
  They had seen the smoke
   and thought there was a fire.
    Then the little boy said,
     'Why don't you stay and watch?'
      So the Fire Department of Popperville
       stayed to watch Mike Mulligan and Mary Anne.
        When they heard the fire engine, the children
         in the school across the street couldn't keep
          their eyes on their lessons. The teacher called
           a long recess and the whole school came out to watch.
            That made Mike Mulligan and Mary Anne
dig still faster and still better.

They finished the second corner neat and square,
but the sun was right up in the top of the sky.

Now the girl who answers
the telephone called up the next towns
of Bangerville and Bopperville and
Kipperville and Kopperville and told them
what was happening in Popperville.
All the people came over to see
if Mike Mulligan and his steam shovel
could dig the cellar in just one day.
The more people came, the faster
Mike Mulligan and Mary Anne dug.
But they would have to hurry.
They were only halfway through
and the sun was beginning
to go down.

They finished the
third corner . . .
neat and square.

31

Never had Mike Mulligan and Mary Anne
had so many people to watch them;
never had they dug so fast and so well;
and never had the sun seemed
to go down so fast.
'Hurry, Mike Mulligan!
Hurry! Hurry!'
shouted the little boy.
'There's not much more time!'
Dirt was flying everywhere,
and the smoke and steam were so thick
that the people could hardly see anything.
But listen!

BING! BANG! CRASH! SLAM!

LOUDER AND LOUDER,

FASTER AND

FASTER.

Then suddenly it was quiet.
Slowly the dirt settled down.
The smoke and steam cleared away,
and there was the cellar
all finished.

Four corners . . . neat and square;
 four walls . . . straight down,
  and Mike Mulligan and Mary Anne at the bottom,
   and the sun was just going down behind the hill.
    'Hurray!' shouted the people. 'Hurray for Mike Mulligan
     and his steam shovel! They have dug the cellar in just one day.'

Suddenly the little boy said,
‘How are they going to get out?’
‘That’s right,’ said Mrs. McGillicuddy
to Henry B. Swap. ‘How is he going
to get his steam shovel out?’
Henry B. Swap didn’t answer,
but he smiled in rather a mean way.
Then everybody said,
‘How are they going to get out?
‘Hi, Mike Mulligan!
How are you going to get
your steam shovel out?’

Mike Mulligan
looked around
at the four square walls
and four square corners,
and he said,
'We've dug so fast
and we've dug so well
that we've quite forgotten
to leave a way out!'
Nothing like this had ever happened
to Mike Mulligan and Mary Anne before,
and they didn't know what to do.

37

Nothing like this
had ever happened before
in Popperville.
Everybody started
talking at once,
and everybody had
a different idea,
and everybody thought
that his idea was the best.
They talked and they talked
and they argued and they fought
till they were worn out,
and still no one knew how to get
Mike Mulligan and Mary Anne
out of the cellar they had dug.
Then Henry B. Swap said,
'The job isn't finished because
Mary Anne isn't out of the cellar,
so Mike Mulligan won't get paid.'
And he smiled again in a rather mean way.

Now the little boy,
who had been keeping very quiet,
had another good idea.
He said,
'Why couldn't we leave Mary Anne in the cellar
and build the new town hall above her?
Let her be the furnace for the new town hall *
and let Mike Mulligan be the janitor.
Then you wouldn't have to buy a new furnace,
and we could pay Mike Mulligan
for digging the cellar
in just one day.'

39

* Acknowledgments to Dickie Birkenbush.

'Why not?' said Henry B. Swap,
 and smiled in a way
  that was not quite so mean.
   'Why not?' said Mrs. McGillicuddy.
   'Why not?' said the Town Constable.
   'Why not?' said all the people.
    So they found a ladder
     and climbed down into the cellar
      to ask Mike Mulligan and Mary Anne.

'Why not?' said Mike Mulligan.
So it was decided,
and everybody was happy.

They built the new town hall
right over Mike Mulligan and Mary Anne.
It was finished before winter.

Every day the little boy goes over to see
Mike Mulligan and Mary Anne,
and Mrs. McGillicuddy takes him
nice hot apple pies. As for Henry B. Swap,
he spends most of his time in the cellar
of the new town hall listening to the stories
that Mike Mulligan has to tell
and smiling in a way that isn't mean at all.

Now when you go to Popperville,
  be sure to go down in the cellar
  of the new town hall.
    There they'll be,
      Mike Mulligan and Mary Anne . . .
      Mike in his rocking chair
      smoking his pipe,
        and Mary Anne beside him,
        warming up the meetings
        in the new town hall.

My first book, Jonnifer Lint, *was about a piece of dust. I and my friends thought it was very clever but thirteen publishers disagreed with us and when I finally got the manuscript back and read it to [my son] Aris, age three and a half, he went to sleep before I could even finish it. That taught me a lesson and from then on I worked with and for my audience, my own children. I would tell them the story over and over, watching their reaction and adjusting to their interest or lack of interest . . . the same with the drawings. Children are very frank critics.*

—Virginia Lee Burton

One such young critic would go on to help the famed author write one of her most enduring picture books.

While visiting a friend, Hazel Albertson, Burton confided that she had a problem with *Mike Mulligan.* She had dug the steam shovel into the town cellar but didn't know how to get her out of it. The solution would come from Albertson's thirteen-year-old grandson, Dick Berkenbush, who was inspired to consider what he might do with a steam shovel stuck in a basement and suggested, "Why not leave it in the cellar for a furnace?"

Two years later, an autographed copy of *Mike Mulligan* arrived in Dick's mailbox. But the book held another surprise in store. Noted with an asterisk next to the phrase "Let her be the furnace for the new town hall," he saw a line that read: "Acknowledgments to Dickie Birkenbush." His last name was misspelled, but he laughed, saying, "We never bothered to change it. I call it my pen name."

Indeed, Burton's work has been written on the hearts of countless readers in picture book masterpieces such as *Maybelle, Katy and the Big Snow, Life Story,* and the Caldecott Medal–winning *The Little House.* Her books are treasured for their timeless themes, satisfying endings, and classic illustrations.

Just as Mike and Mary Anne helped carve out a new America, Virginia Lee Burton's words and pictures continue to pave the way toward a life-long love of books for millions of young readers and their families.

Collect all of these Virginia Lee Burton classics: